Hansel and Gretel

Adapted by Amanda Askew
Illustrated by Andy Catling

QED
QED Publishing

Once upon a time, Hansel and Gretel lived in a
tiny cottage with their father, a poor woodcutter,
and their cruel stepmother.

"There are too many mouths to feed,"
their stepmother told the woodcutter.
"Take the children miles from home, so far
that they can never find their way back!"

Overhearing the conversation, Hansel slipped
out of the house, filled his pockets with
pebbles and then went back to bed.

All night long, the woodcutter's wife went on at her husband. The next day, he led Hansel and Gretel away into the forest.

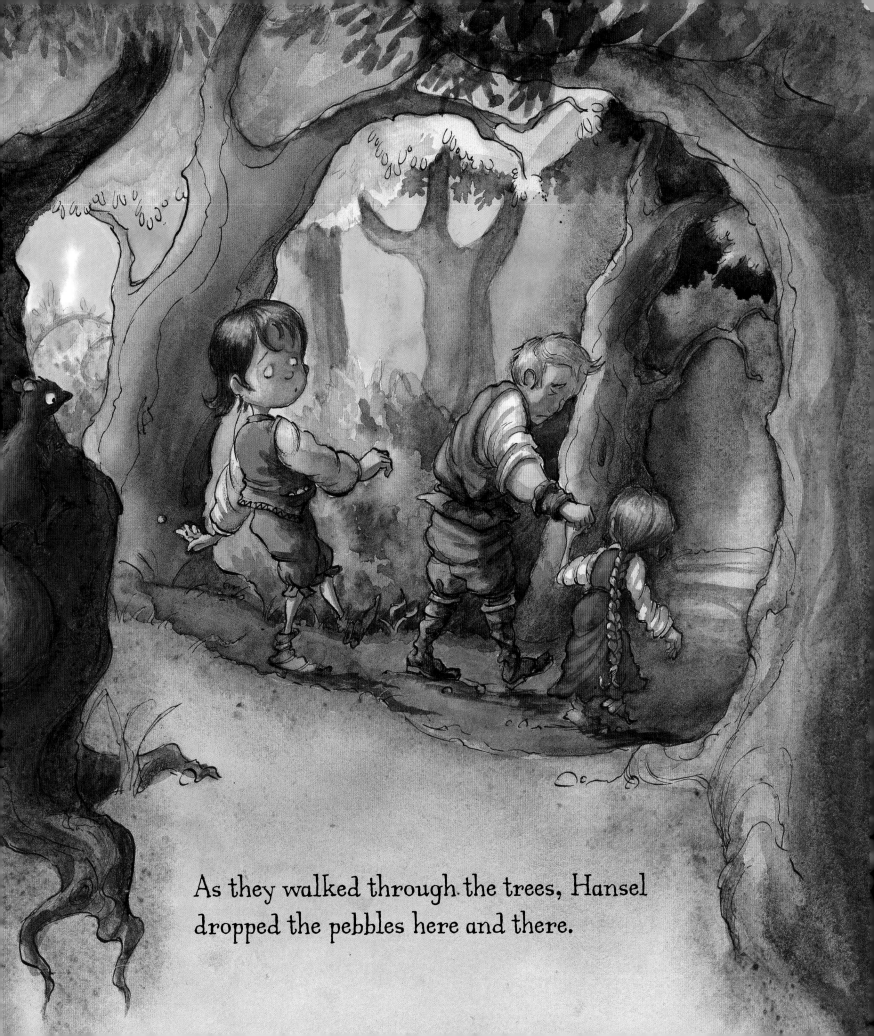

As they walked through the trees, Hansel
dropped the pebbles here and there.

Suddenly, the children found themselves
alone as the woodcutter slipped away.
Gretel began to sob bitterly.

"Don't cry. I'll take you home, even if Father
doesn't come back for us!"

Luckily the moon was full that night, and
the pebbles gleamed in the moonlight.

The children found their way home and crept through a half-open window, without wakening their parents.

When their stepmother discovered that Hansel
and Gretel had returned, she was mad.

She kept Hansel and Gretel under lock and key
all day, with only a sip of water and stale bread.

When dawn came, the woodcutter led the
children out into the forest once again.

Hansel, however, had not eaten his bread,
and as he walked through the trees, he left
a trail of crumbs to mark the way.

Again, the children found themselves alone.

"Don't worry. I've left a trail, like last time," Hansel whispered to Gretel.

Sadly, the little boy had forgotten about the hungry animals in the forest. In no time at all, the crumbs had all been eaten.

When dawn broke, they wandered through the forest. On and on they walked, till they came upon a strange cottage.

"This is chocolate!" gasped Hansel as he broke a lump of plaster from the wall.

"And this is icing!" exclaimed Gretel, putting a piece of pillar in her mouth.

Starving but delighted, the children began to eat pieces of the cottage.

Quietly, the biscuit door swung open.
There stood an old woman.

"Well, well," said the old woman, peering at them. "Haven't you children got a sweet tooth? Come in and eat what you wish."

Unluckily for Hansel and Gretel, the sweetie cottage belonged to a witch. They had fallen into her trap.

"You're nothing but skin and bones," cried the witch, locking Hansel into a cage. "I shall fatten you up and eat you!"

"You will do the housework," she told Gretel. "Then I'll make a meal of you, too!"

Each day, the witch would feel Hansel's finger.
The witch had poor eyesight, so he held out a chicken bone.

"Too thin!" she complained.
"When will you become plump?"

One day the witch grew tired of waiting...

"Light the oven," she told Gretel. "We're going to have roasted boy today!"

When the witch bent down to see if the oven was hot enough, Gretel gave her a tremendous push and slammed the oven door shut.

Free at last, the children stayed at the cottage, eating sweets. After a few days, they found a huge chocolate egg, filled with gold coins.

"The witch is now burnt to a cinder," said Hansel. "We'll take the treasure home with us, to Father."

They set off into the forest and on the second day, they found their way home. Their wicked stepmother left in disgust, so Hansel, Gretel and their father lived happily ever after.

Notes for parents and teachers

- Look at the front cover of the book together. Can the children guess what the story might be about? Read the title together. Does this give them more of a clue?

- When the children first read the story or you read it together, can they guess what might happen in the end?

- What do the children think of the characters? Is the stepmother kind? What about Father? Should the witch have been put in the oven? Who is their favourite character and why?

- The villains in this story are the stepmother and the witch. Can the children think of any other stories with similar characters?

- When Hansel and Gretel meet the witch, do the children think they will escape? Are the children glad that Hansel and Gretel go home at the end of the story?

- What would the children do if they found a cottage made of sweets? Ask the children to draw or paint their own 'sweetie' house.

- What other endings can the children think of? Perhaps the children can act out the story, and then the new endings.

- Hansel and Gretel look after each other. Do the children have any siblings? Do they look after each other?

Copyright © QED Publishing 2010

First published in the UK in 2010 by
QED Publishing
A Quarto Group Company
226 City Road
London EC1V 2TT

www.qed-publishing.co.uk

ISBN 978 1 84835 488 3

Printed in China

A catalogue record for this book is available from the British Library.

Editor: Amanda Askew
Designers: Vida and Luke Kelly